If You're Happy and You Know it!

adapted by Anna McQuinn

illustrated by Sophie Fatus

Barefoot Books
Celebrating Art and Story

If you're happy and you know it, clap your hands!
If you're happy and you know it, clap your hands!
If you're happy and you know it,
and you really want to show it,
If you're happy and you know it,
clap your hands!

If you're happy and you know it,
and you really want to show it,

If you're happy and you know it,
stamp your feet!
If you're happy and
you know it, stamp your feet!

If you're happy and you know it,
stamp your feet!

If you're happy and you know it, turn around!
If you're happy and you know it, turn around!
If you're happy and you know it, and you really want to show it,
If you're happy and you know it, turn around!

If you're happy and you know it, wiggle your hips!
If you're happy and you know it, wiggle your hips!
If you're happy and you know it, and you really want to show it,
If you're happy and you know it, wiggle your hips!

If you're happy and you know it, stretch your arms!
If you're happy and you know it, stretch your arms!
If you're happy and you know it, and you really want to show it,

If you're happy and you know it, stretch your arms!

If you're happy and you know it, pat your head!
If you're happy and you know it, pat your head!
If you're happy and you know it, and you really want to show it,
If you're happy and you know it, pat your head!

If you're happy and you know it, touch your nose!
If you're happy and you know it, touch your nose!
If you're happy and you know it, and you really want to show it,
If you're happy and you know it, touch your nose!

If you're happy and you know it, point your toes!
If you're happy and you know it, point your toes!
If you're happy and you know it, and you really want to show it,
If you're happy and you know it, point your toes!

If you're happy and you know it, shout hello!
If you're happy and you know it, shout hello!
If you're happy and you know it, and you really want to show it,
If you're happy and you know it, shout hello!

"Merhaba"

"Han, mish'ke"

"Hola"

"Selam"

"Hello"

"Hallo"

"Dia dhuit"

"Dag"

"Senga yai"

"Geia sou"

"Salaam"

"G'day"

"Hoi"

"Kahé"

"Saukhyama"

"Oi"

"Ai"

"Moikka"

Aurélie
France

Ming Hoa
China (Mandarin)

Lulu
Tanzania

Omar
Pakistan

Konrad
Poland

Simran
India (Hindi)

Fetsum
Ethiopia

Fatima
Malaysia

Sukhinder
India (Punjabi)

Sasha
Russia

Annette
Austria

Oisín
Ireland

Arina
Afghanistan

Shota
N. America (Lako

Zainab
Lebanon

Calida
Greece

Pedro
Portugal

Bente
The Netherland

Himari
Japan

Vittorio
Italy

Robindra
Bangladesh

Muna
Somalia

Jubulani
Zimbabwe

Sōng
China (Cantonese)

Raúl
Spain

Nkem
Nigeria

Kajarithan
Sri Lanka

Yeab
Eritrea

Hanne
Germany

Mehmet
Turkey

Ben
Canada

Yasbet
Mexico

Saimi
Finland

Arapoosh
N. America (Apsaaloke)

Shane
Australia

Kirima
Canada (Inukitut)

If You're Happy and You Know it!

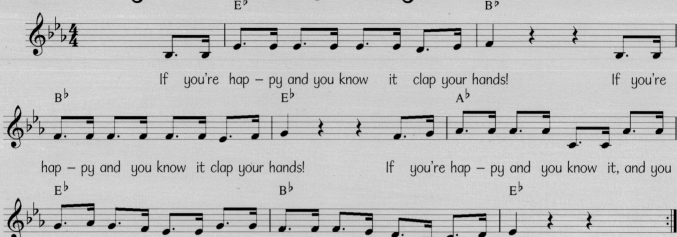

If you're hap – py and you know it clap your hands! If you're

hap – py and you know it clap your hands! If you're hap – py and you know it, and you

real – ly want to show it, if you're hap–py and you know it, clap your hands!

Barefoot Books
124 Walcot Street
Bath, BA1 5BG

Adaption copyright © 2009 by Anna McQuinn
Illustrations copyright © 2009 by Sophie Fatus
The moral right of Anna McQuinn to be identified as the author and
Sophie Fatus to be identified as the illustrator of this work has been asserted

First published in Great Britain by Barefoot Books, Ltd
and in the United States of America by Barefoot Books, Inc. in 2009
This paperback edition published in 2010. All rights reserved
Graphic design by Louise Millar, London. Reproduction by Grafiscan, Verona
Printed and bound on 100% acid-free paper in Singapore by Tien Wah Press, Ltd
This book was typeset in Neu Phollick Alpha & Circus Dog
The illustrations were prepared in acrylics

Paperback ISBN 978-1-84686-434-6

Library of Congress Cataloging-in-Publication Data is available under LCCN 2008039827
British Cataloguing-in-Publication Data:
a catalogue record for this book is available from the British Library

3 5 7 9 8 6 4 2

TESTING IT: AN OFF-THE-SHELF SOFTWARE TESTING PROCESS, 2ND EDITION

Testing IT provides a complete, off-the-shelf software testing process framework for any testing practitioner who is looking to research, implement, roll out, adopt, and maintain a software testing process. It covers all aspects of testing for software developed or modified in-house, modified or extended legacy systems, and software developed by a third party. Software professionals can customize the framework to match the testing requirements of any organization, and six real-world testing case studies are provided to show how other organizations have done this. Packed with a series of real-world case studies, the book also provides a comprehensive set of downloadable testing document templates, proformas, and checklists to support the process of customizing. This new edition demonstrates the role and use of agile testing best practices and includes a specific agile case study.

John Watkins has more than thirty years of experience in the field of software development, with some twenty-five years in the field of software testing. During his career, John has been involved at all levels and phases of testing and has provided high-level test process consultancy, training, and mentoring to numerous blue chip companies.

He is both a Chartered IT Professional and a Fellow of the British Computer Society, where he is an active member of the Specialist Group in Software Testing (SIGiST), previously serving on committees of the Intellect Testing Group (representing the U.K. technology industry) and the SmallTalk User Group.

He is the author of *Agile Testing: How to Succeed in an Extreme Testing Environment* and currently works for IBM's software group.

Simon Mills has more than thirty years of experience in the field of software quality, having transferred into the world of system testing from a business role. Simon has been involved in testing software in both business and technical or scientific environments from major investment and insurance systems to laser control, cryogenic control, and superconducting applications. He is the founder of Ingenuity System Testing Services, the preeminent testing authority in the field of electronically traded insurance in the United Kingdom.

Simon is widely published internationally in conference proceedings, papers, and contributions to books and has presented as an invited speaker in the United States, at EuroStar, and at the World Congress for Software Quality.